DISNEY
MULAN

Adapted by Gina Ingoglia
Drawings by José Cardona
Painted by Don Williams

 A GOLDEN BOOK • NEW YORK

rhcbooks.com
ISBN 978-0-7364-3053-1 (trade) — ISBN 978-0-385-38900-6 (ebook)
Printed in the United States of America
20 19 18 17 16 15 14 13

Like a powerful dragon, the Great Wall of China winds its way across the land. It protects the country's farmland and villages, its family temples, and the miles of bright-green rice paddies. All along the wall, soldiers stand guard. They don't suspect that this great barrier is about to be crossed by an army of Huns led by the ferocious Shan-Yu. . . .

One afternoon, a young woman named Mulan sadly returned home from the village. Making a good marriage was the way a young Chinese woman brought honor to her family, but Mulan's meeting with the Matchmaker that morning had ended in disaster.

Her father, Fa Zhou, sat with her. With kind, loving words, he assured his daughter that she, like the late-blooming blossom that proves to be the most beautiful of all, would bring honor to the family in her own time.

BOOM! BOOM! BOOM! Suddenly, a loud drum summoned everyone out of their homes.

"The Huns have invaded China!" a messenger announced. "One man from every family must serve in the Imperial Army."

When the Fa family was called, Fa Zhou handed his cane
to his wife and stepped forward.

"No!" cried Mulan. She knew her father was as brave as he
had been in his youth, but he was no longer strong. He would
never survive a war.

It rained hard that night. Mulan went to the family temple, lit incense, and prayed to her Ancestors.

She made her decision. She would take her father's place.

Mulan took Fa Zhou's sword and cut her hair short. Then she put on his armor. Disguised as a man, she rode her horse, Khan, into the storm.

A tiny dragon named Mushu raced after her. He wanted to regain his position as a Guardian of the Fa family. "I'll make Mulan a hero! That will show the Ancestors!" he said.

A lucky cricket named Cri-Kee hopped along beside him.

Mulan wasn't sure what to think about Mushu and Cri-Kee. But she knew she needed all the help she could get.

When Mulan reached the army camp, she reported to Captain Shang. Shang was the son of General Li, leader of the Emperor's army. It was Shang's job to train the new recruits to be good soldiers.

"What's your name?" Shang asked.

Mulan made up a boy's name. "P-Ping . . . ," she stammered. "My name is Ping."

The recruits had trouble with the training exercises. The most difficult test was retrieving an arrow from the top of a tall column. No recruit had been able to do it. Clever Mulan finally figured out how to use strength and discipline to get the arrow.

Everyone cheered.

One evening, Mushu and Cri-Kee overheard
Chi Fu, the Emperor's aide, talking to Shang.
"Your troops will never see battle," he said.
"This guy is messing with my plan," said
Mushu. "I think it is time we took this war
into our own hands."

So Cri-Kee and Mushu put on a clever disguise and delivered a note to Chi Fu. The note read, *You and your men are needed at the front at once!*

Shang set out immediately with his troops. Soon they came across a burned-out village that had been attacked by the Huns.

"We must go to the Imperial City," he said. "We are the only hope for the Emperor now."

The men trudged on.

Suddenly, hundreds of flaming arrows flew down at them. Shan-Yu's Hun army was charging toward Shang and his men!

"Fire the cannons!" yelled Shang. Soon only one cannon was left.
Mulan looked up at the snowy mountain peak and got an idea.
She grabbed the last cannon and fired. The cannonball slammed into
the mountain and shook the snow loose. An avalanche thundered
down and swept the enemy away!

Mulan leapt onto her horse and raced across the snow to Shang, who lay unconscious. She lifted him onto Khan's strong back. Khan skidded dangerously on the steep slope, but the other soldiers helped pull them to safety.

When Shang came to, he noticed that Mulan had been wounded. She was taken to the medic's tent.

Later, the army medic reported startling news: Ping was a woman! Serving in the army as a woman was a crime punishable by death.

Shang spared Mulan because she had saved him. "A life for a life," he said.

The troops marched off, leaving Mulan behind with Khan, Mushu, and Cri-Kee.

Mulan was about to head home in disgrace. But then she saw Shan-Yu and five of his soldiers at the top of a cliff, heading toward the Imperial City. They were still alive!

Mulan and Khan galloped off to the city. There she found Shang and told him that the Huns were on their way.

Still feeling betrayed, Shang did not believe her.

Later, during the victory ceremony, Shan-Yu captured the Emperor. Mulan saw Shang frantically trying to break into the palace.

"I've got an idea," she called.

Mulan dressed her three soldier friends, Yao, Ling, and Chien-Po, in women's clothes so that they could fool the Hun guards. Shang followed them, and they overpowered the guards.

On a palace balcony, Shan-Yu waved his sword at the Emperor. "Bow to me!" he demanded.

At Mulan's signal, the rescuers stormed into the room.

The Emperor was taken to safety. Shan-Yu was furious.
He charged toward Mulan.

Mulan rushed to Mushu and told him her plan. She sent
him off with Cri-Kee to the fireworks tower.

Mulan ran through the palace, making sure Shan-Yu was
following her. Then she led him onto the roof.

Using her speed and strength, Mulan pinned
Shan-Yu's cloak to the roof with his own sword!

Mushu arrived with a lit rocket and jumped
away just as it crashed into the villain.

KABOOM! A spectacular fireworks
explosion dazzled the city.

Shan-Yu was no more.

Mulan approached the Emperor.

"You have saved us all," he said, bowing to her. He asked Mulan to join his council, but Mulan chose to go home to her family. "Then take this so your family will know what you have done for me," he said as he placed his pendant around her neck.

Soon Mulan was back at home, enjoying a happy reunion with her family, when Shang arrived. He had realized that Mulan was a very special person indeed.

Mushu was a Guardian once more!

Mulan had brought honor to her family, the Ancestors, and all of China.